THE U.S. NATIONAL GUARD

★ INSIDE THE U.S. MILITARY ★

Rosen Publishing

BY TANNER BILLINGS

Library of Congress Cataloging-in-Publication Data

Names: Billings, Tanner, author.
Title: The U.S. National Guard / Tanner Billings.
Description: New York : Rosen Publishing, [2022] | Series: Inside the U.S. military | Includes index. | Contents: Get to Know the Guard -- History of the Guard -- On the Job -- National Guard Values.
Identifiers: LCCN 2020006177 | ISBN 9781978518674 (library binding) | ISBN 9781978518667 (paperback) | ISBN 9781978518681 (ebook)
Subjects: LCSH: United States--National Guard--Juvenile literature.
Classification: LCC UA42 .B47 2022 | DDC 355.3/70973--dc23
LC record available at https://lccn.loc.gov/2020006177

First Edition

Published in 2022 by The Rosen Publishing Group, Inc.
29 East 21st Street, New York, NY 10010

Copyright © 2022 Rosen Publishing

Designer: Sarah Liddell
Editor: Kate Mikoley

Photo credits: Cover, background used throughout Dakin/Shutterstock.com; p. 4 CAITLIN O'HARA/Contributor/AFP/Getty Images; p. 5 Star Tribune via Getty Images/Contributor/Star Tribune/Getty Images; pp. 7, 8 Joe Raedle/Staff/Getty Images News/Getty Images; p. 10 Rob Lewine/Getty Images; p. 12 Clindberg/Wikimedia Commons; p. 14 MCT/Contributor/Tribune News Service/Getty Images; p. 15 George Frey/Stringer/Getty Images News/Getty Images; p. 17 Kwwhit5531/Wikimedia Commons; p. 19 Steven Clevenger/Contributor/Getty Images; p. 21 MediaNews Group/Orange County Register via Getty Images/Contributor/MediaNews Group/Getty Images; p. 23 Futurhit12/Wikimedia Commons; p. 25 PictureLake/iStock/Getty Images Plus/Getty Images; p. 27 Smith Collection/Gado/Contributor/Archive Photos/Getty Images; p. 30 Gregory Primus/500Px Plus/Getty Images; p. 34 milehightraveler/iStock Unreleased/Getty Images; p. 38 Fæ/Wikimedia Commons; p. 40 Erich Schlegel/Stringer/Getty Images News/Getty Images; p. 42 Scott Olson/Staff/Getty Images News/Getty Images; p. 44 Sean Murphy/Image Source/Getty Images.

All rights reserved. No part of this book may be reproduced in any form without permission in writing from the publisher, except by a reviewer.

Printed in the United States of America

Some of the images in this book illustrate individuals who are models. The depictions do not imply actual situations or events.

CPSIA compliance information: Batch #BSRYA22: For further information contact Rosen Publishing, New York, New York at 1-800-237-9932.

Find us on f ⓘ

CONTENTS

Serving the Nation 4

Chapter One: Get to Know the Guard . . . 6

Chapter Two: History of the Guard 16

Chapter Three: On the Job 26

Chapter Four: National Guard Values . . . 36

Glossary 46

For More Information 47

Index 48

Words in the glossary appear in **bold** type
the first time they are used in the text.

SERVING THE NATION

Within the U.S. military are five armed forces: the army, navy, air force, coast guard, and Marine **Corps**. A sixth force, the U.S. National Guard, is a bit different from these other forces. Members of the national guard serve both their country and their local communities.

THE NATIONAL GUARD IS PART OF THE MILITARY'S RESERVE FORCES, OR FORCES MADE UP OF SOLDIERS WHO AREN'T PART OF THE MAIN FORCES, BUT MAY BE CALLED TO **ACTIVE DUTY** IF NEEDED.

While the national guard is often referred to as one single force, it's actually made up of two forces: the army national guard and the air national guard. The air national guard is a part of the air force, while the army national guard is part of the army. While both are part of the U.S. National Guard, each serves a somewhat different mission.

CHAPTER ONE: GET TO KNOW THE GUARD

Every state and territory in the United States has its own national guard. For the most part, a soldier in the guard works in their home state. Members of the guard follow orders from the governor of their state. They can be deployed to communities facing all kinds of emergencies, such as **natural disasters** or large acts of violence. Most of the time, when national guardsmen are called into duty, it's to a place within their home state. However, at times of national or major emergencies, they may be sent to other states. This commonly happens during destructive natural disasters, such as **hurricanes**.

DEPLOY: TO MOVE TROOPS INTO A POSITION OF READINESS

GUARDSMAN: A PERSON SERVING IN THE NATIONAL GUARD

MEMBERS OF THE NATIONAL GUARD ARE OFTEN SENT TO AREAS TO HELP PEOPLE DURING OR AFTER BIG NATURAL DISASTERS, SUCH AS FLOODS.

At times, members of the national guard also take orders from the president. During war or other national emergencies, the president may send the national guard overseas to fight for their country. When this happens, it means the members are called to active duty. While being in the national guard is generally a part-time job, and not an active-duty position, people enlisting need to consider the fact that they can be called to fight full-time as an active-duty soldier for up to two years.

PEOPLE WHO HAVE SERVED ON ACTIVE DUTY OR IN ANOTHER MILITARY BRANCH DON'T HAVE TO MEET ALL THE SAME REQUIREMENTS AS NEW ENLISTEES. FOR EXAMPLE, THEY MAY BE OLDER THAN 35 OR 39.

WHO CAN SERVE?

Guardsmen need to be tough, mentally and physically. They also need to be driven and work well with a team. To enlist in the army national guard, you must be between 17 and 35. To join the air national guard, you must be between 17 and 39. If you're 17, you need permission from a parent or guardian. You can enlist in the air national guard as a senior in high school, but you can't begin training until you've finished high school or received your **GED**. Those enlisting also need to be able to pass certain tests and screenings.

ENLIST: TO SIGN UP FOR DUTY IN THE MILITARY

Those joining the National Guard need to be a certain height and weight and meet certain fitness standards.

Those serving in the guard commonly hold other jobs or go to college while taking part in their part-time military training. When not called to duty by either the governor or the president, members of the national guard generally have to report for one training weekend a month. Both the air national guard and army national guard also require members to complete a two-week training session each year.

★ EXPLORE MORE ★

IN THE ARMY NATIONAL GUARD, A 17-YEAR-OLD WITH PERMISSION FROM A PARENT OR GUARDIAN CAN TAKE PART IN BASIC TRAINING ACTIVITIES BETWEEN THEIR JUNIOR AND SENIOR YEARS OF HIGH SCHOOL. THEY CAN'T TAKE PART IN ADVANCED TRAINING UNTIL THEY'VE FINISHED HIGH SCHOOL.

A PERSON IN THE AIR NATIONAL GUARD COMMITS TO SERVE AT LEAST SIX YEARS.

A person can sign up to serve in the army national guard for as short a time as three years. However, they're committed to serving a total of eight years. The rest can be served in the Individual Ready Reserve. This means you won't have to train regularly with a unit, but can still be called to duty in an emergency.

ACING THE ASVAB

Before a person can enter the U.S. armed forces, they must take the Armed Services Vocational Aptitude Battery, or ASVAB. This is a test that involves using many different skills in subjects such as math and English. Test takers must earn a certain score on the ASVAB to be able to join the national guard. How a person does on certain sections of the test also helps decide what kinds of jobs in the guard would be a good fit for them. Those entering both the air and army national guards take the ASVAB.

 EXPLORE MORE

THE FIRST STEP TO JOINING BOTH THE AIR AND ARMY NATIONAL GUARDS IS OFTEN MEETING WITH A RECRUITER. THIS IS A PERSON WHOSE JOB IT IS TO HELP PEOPLE SIGN UP FOR THE MILITARY. THEY CAN ANSWER ANY QUESTIONS A PERSON MIGHT HAVE BEFORE THEY JOIN.

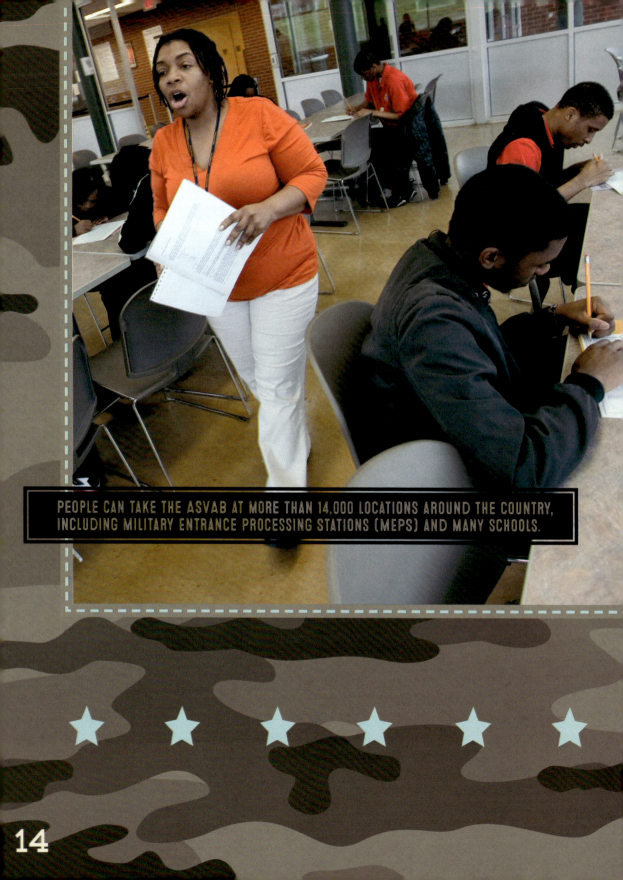

People can take the ASVAB at more than 14,000 locations around the country, including Military Entrance Processing Stations (MEPS) and many schools.

Members of the national guard have to be ready to defend and protect their country whenever needed. Although they are a part-time force, their duty can become full-time at any time. National guard forces can respond to emergencies around the world in fewer than two days. In times of local or stateside emergency, these forces can arrive much quicker, often within just a few hours.

CHAPTER TWO: HISTORY OF THE GUARD

The history of the national guard dates back to long before the United States was even its own country! On December 13, 1636, the first **militia** units in North America were organized to defend the Massachusetts Bay Colony. Colonists brought the idea for militias with them from England. These military units were organized by the citizens to protect themselves, their families, and their local communities from attacks. Colonists formed three militia units to protect the Massachusetts Bay Colony in this way. Today, December 13 is celebrated as the birthday of the army national guard.

THIS PAINTING, CALLED *THE FIRST MUSTER* BY DON TROIANI, SHOWS THE FIRST GATHERING OF ONE OF THE MILITIA UNITS IN THE MASSACHUSETTS BAY COLONY.

17

★ EXPLORE MORE ★

THE 181ST INFANTRY, 182ND INFANTRY, 101ST FIELD **ARTILLERY**, AND 101ST ENGINEER BATTALION IN TODAY'S MASSACHUSETTS ARMY NATIONAL GUARD ARE THE OLDEST UNITS IN THE U.S. MILITARY. THEY DESCEND FROM THE FIRST MILITIA UNITS IN THE MASSACHUSETTS BAY COLONY.

INFANTRY: SOLDIERS TRAINED TO FIGHT ON FOOT

While not formally organized by the government as today's military is, the oldest of the colonial militias are still considered the oldest units in the U.S. military. By 1916, the units had become more formally organized and the force took on the name it still carries today—the national guard.

IN RECENT YEARS, MANY MEMBERS OF THE NATIONAL GUARD HAVE BEEN DEPLOYED OVERSEAS TO COUNTRIES SUCH AS AFGHANISTAN AND IRAQ.

BATTALION: A LARGE, ORGANIZED GROUP OF SOLDIERS, COMMONLY MADE UP OF COMMANDERS AND TWO COMPANIES

★ EXPLORE MORE ★

FROM THE MILITIAMEN WHO PROTECTED THEIR HOMES IN THE LATE 1600S TO THE PEOPLE SERVING MORE RECENTLY, MEMBERS OF THE NATIONAL GUARD HAVE TAKEN PART IN EVERY MAJOR CONFLICT IN AMERICAN HISTORY.

Each year, the air national guard celebrates its birthday on September 18. On that date in 1947, the air force officially broke away from the U.S. Army and became its own separate part of the military. Before then, the U.S. Army Air Forces, under the direction and authority of the army, performed air force duties. There were several national guard units that performed similar tasks as today's air national guard, but they were still part of the army. The National Security Act of 1947 allowed for formation of a separate U.S. Air Force, which also included the air national guard.

THE NATIONAL GUARD HAS SEVERAL BANDS THAT PERFORM AT PARADES AND OTHER EVENTS.

21

ALWAYS READY, ALWAYS THERE

The official song of the National Guard **Bureau** is called "Always Ready, Always There." Its lyrics recognize the importance of both the soldiers and the airmen who serve in the national guard. The first few lines of the song are:

> We are the Guard,
> Soldiers and Airmen all prepared.
> We are the National Guard,
> we serve on land and in the air.

The song mentions that a guardsman's duty is served both at home and around the world, but no matter what, as the song says, the guard is "Always Ready, Always There."

AIRMAN: A PERSON IN THE AIR FORCE

THE TITLE OF THE NATIONAL GUARD SONG, "ALWAYS READY, ALWAYS THERE," IS ALSO COMMONLY USED AS A MOTTO FOR THE GUARD. IT'S SHOWN HERE ON THE NATIONAL GUARD SEAL.

Although September 18, 1947, is considered the official start date of the air national guard, its real beginnings came earlier. While the air force was under the authority of the army, units that would eventually become part of what's now known as the air national guard were organized. For example, in 1915, the New York National Guard authorized a unit called the Aero Company, Signal Corps. Now known as the 102nd Rescue Squadron of the New York Air National Guard, it's the oldest unit in the air national guard. The national guard included 59 **aviation** units at the time of the air force's creation. Each of these units was officially part of the new air force by April 27, 1948.

109TH AIRLIFT SQUADRON

The oldest unit in the air national guard that's continuously existed since its formation is the 109th Airlift Squadron of the Minnesota Air National Guard. In its early days, the unit was known as the 109th Observation Squadron. It became an official unit on January 17, 1921. It was the first air unit in the national guard to be recognized by the country's federal, or central, government after World War I (1914–1918). Soon, more units joined the U.S. Army Air Corps, which would become part of the U.S. Army Air Forces that served in World War II (1939–1945).

Although a lot has changed about the national guard since it started, it's still an important force for keeping Americans protected at home.

THE STAMP SHOWN HERE WAS RELEASED IN 1953 TO HONOR THE WORK OF THE U.S. NATIONAL GUARD.

CHAPTER THREE: ON THE JOB

Members of the national guard have many jobs to choose from. Of course, when considering joining the guard, one of the first choices one must make is whether to serve in the air national guard or the army national guard. The air force's job is to defend the country in the air, while the army's job is to defend it on land.

After deciding which of the two forces one wants to serve in, there are still lots of job choices. The air national guard has more than 200 job fields to pick from. The army national guard has more than 150 different jobs for those who join.

WHILE THE NATIONAL GUARD IS COMMONLY CONTROLLED AND ORGANIZED BY THE INDIVIDUAL STATES, IT'S STILL PART OF THE NATIONAL MILITARY AND RECEIVES FUNDING FROM THE FEDERAL GOVERNMENT.

THE BASICS OF BASIC

Anyone joining the national guard who hasn't previously served in the military must complete basic training, commonly just called basic. New members of the air national guard, called recruits, go to Air Force Basic Military Training at Lackland Air Force Base in Texas. This training is about eight and a half weeks long. Army national guard recruits attend a basic training that lasts for 10 weeks. Both trainings are tough and include many mental and physical challenges to help recruits gain skills they'll need to succeed in the guard. After basic, it's time for Advanced Individual Training (AIT). Here, people learn key skills related to their specific position with the guard.

A MEMBER OF THE U.S. ARMY'S JOB IS KNOWN AS THEIR "MILITARY OCCUPATIONAL SPECIALTY," OR MOS. EACH JOB IS KNOWN BY A CODE, SUCH AS 89B FOR **AMMUNITION** SPECIALIST. SIMILARLY, THE AIR FORCE HAS "AIR FORCE SPECIALTY CODES," OR AFSCs.

ARMY NATIONAL GUARD BASIC TRAINING

RED PHASE
During weeks one through three, recruits begin physical training. They learn to follow orders and conduct themselves as soldiers. They also get an introduction to the Army's values and traditions.

WHITE PHASE
In weeks four and five, recruits continue their physical training and learn how to use a gun and practice shooting at targets.

BLUE PHASE
In weeks six through nine, recruits receive advanced weapons training and field training. They are tested on the many skills they have learned.

Army National Guard basic training includes three phases, or stages. In the tenth week of training, recruits spend time with their families and graduate!

Since flying is a big part of the air force's mission, you might think there would be a lot of pilots in the air national guard. While there are some, most people in the force work primarily on the ground. Plenty of these jobs still involve working on aircraft though. People, such as mechanics, are needed to help maintain the aircraft. Others perform reconnaissance and have a part in special operations.

AIR GUARDSMEN USE THE LATEST TECHNOLOGY WHEN WORKING BOTH ON THE GROUND AND IN THE AIR.

RECONNAISSANCE: THE EXPLORATION OF A PLACE TO COLLECT INFORMATION

Without the air guardsmen on the ground, many of the tasks the force completes in the air would not be able to happen. Weather units work on finding the most precise forecasts to keep the guard safe both in the sky and on the ground. Guardsmen are also needed to help train recruits.

Another key field in the air national guard is air traffic control. Like the name suggests, people in this field control the traffic in the airspace they're in charge of. This can be around 50,000 square miles (129,500 sq km)! These members of the guard are in charge of keeping the air and surrounding ground area safe. This can involve tracking aircraft, studying routes, and keeping track of vehicles in the air and on the ground.

VEHICLE: AN OBJECT USED FOR CARRYING OR TRANSPORTING PEOPLE OR GOODS, SUCH AS A CAR, TRUCK, OR AIRPLANE

BECOMING AN OFFICER

Enlisted soldiers or airmen make up the majority of the guard, but like other military forces, the national guard needs officers too. In the army national guard, officers fall into two groups: warrant and commissioned officers. Warrant officers are experts in their field and serve as leaders in a special area, while commissioned officers have broader roles. In the air national guard, rated officers are commissioned officers in positions involving flying, such as pilots. Commissioned officers without flying-related jobs are non-rated officers. Non-commissioned officers are officers who have risen through the ranks and been promoted to higher levels of responsibility without a direct commission.

INTELLIGENCE: THE GATHERING OF SECRET INFORMATION ABOUT ENEMIES, POSSIBLE ENEMIES, AND THE AREAS THEY'RE INVOLVED IN

★ EXPLORE MORE ★

When deployed overseas, members of the National Guard may go into combat positions. However, they're commonly sent on other types of missions, such as those involving building schools or hospitals, and training locals on peacekeeping skills.

Some of the jobs in the army national guard are similar to those in the air national guard. In fact, some army national guardsmen even work in air defense. Both guards need people to work in medical, police, and other emergency-response positions. There are also many jobs in STEM—or science, technology, engineering, and math—fields. Some people in the guard work in intelligence. Others work on weapons and make sure guardsmen are properly armed if they need to enter battle.

HELICOPTER PILOTS IN THE ARMY NATIONAL GUARD LEARN HOW TO FLY ALL SORTS OF ADVANCED AIRCRAFT, LIKE THIS UH-60 BLACK HAWK.

MILITARY PHONETIC ALPHABET

A: ALPHA
B: BRAVO
C: CHARLIE
D: DELTA
E: ECHO
F: FOXTROT
G: GOLF
H: HOTEL
I: INDIA
J: JULIET
K: KILO
L: LIMA
M: MIKE

N: NOVEMBER
O: OSCAR
P: PAPA
Q: QUEBEC
R: ROMEO
S: SIERRA
T: TANGO
U: UNIFORM
V: VICTOR
W: WHISKEY
X: XRAY
Y: YANKEE
Z: ZULU

MEMBERS OF THE MILITARY LEARN TO USE WORDS TO REPRESENT LETTERS WHEN SPEAKING OVER THE RADIO. CALLED THE PHONETIC ALPHABET, THIS HELPS AVOID MISUNDERSTANDINGS.

CHAPTER FOUR: NATIONAL GUARD VALUES

Members of the national guard need to be strong mentally and physically. They also need to be hardworking and committed to serving their country both in times of war and times of peace.

FOR A LONG TIME, WOMEN WEREN'T ALLOWED TO HOLD OFFICIAL POSITIONS IN THE MILITARY. TODAY, ABOUT 10 PERCENT OF ALL U.S. MILITARY VETERANS ARE WOMEN.

VETERAN: SOMEONE WHO HAS SERVED IN THE MILITARY

WOMEN IN THE GUARD

The first woman to join the air national guard was Captain Norma Parsons in 1956. She was part of the New York Air National Guard. The following year, in January 1957, First Lieutenant Sylvia Marie St. Charles Law became the first woman in the army national guard when she joined the Alabama Army National Guard. While these were big steps for women in the military, there were still many limitations on the jobs women could hold. Until 1967, the only women allowed to serve in the guard were officers in medical positions.

IN 2019, BRIGADIER GENERAL LAURA YEAGER BECAME THE FIRST WOMAN TO LEAD A U.S. ARMY INFANTRY DIVISION WHEN SHE TOOK COMMAND OF THE 40TH INFANTRY DIVISION IN THE CALIFORNIA NATIONAL GUARD.

BRIGADIER GENERAL: AN OFFICER IN THE MILITARY WHO IS RANKED ABOVE A COLONEL

Each branch of the military has its own values and ideals. As part of the army, the army national guard follows that branch's values.

The seven core, or central, values of the army are loyalty, duty, respect, selfless service, honor, integrity, and personal courage.

Loyalty means being faithful and supportive. Soldiers are loyal to both their country and their fellow soldiers. Duty means carrying out and completing all tasks to the best of your ability. Respect means treating everyone how they should be treated. Selfless service means putting the needs of your country and of others before your own. Honor is respect that is earned by living up to all the army's values. Integrity involves being fair and honest. It means always doing what is right—legally and morally. Personal courage means facing your fears, **adversity**, and danger.

When a member of the National Guard goes to a dangerous area to help those in need, they are performing selfless service.

THE SERVICE: ANOTHER TERM FOR A COUNTRY'S MILITARY FORCES

BENEFITS

Many active duty military members live on bases. These are often similar to regular towns and usually include housing, stores, gyms, schools, and entertainment facilities such as movie theaters. National guardsmen who have not been called to active duty do not live on bases, but as members of the service, they are allowed to go to the bases and use these facilities. There are other perks to being in the guard too. For example, the military can help members earn college degrees. Joining the guard can be a great way to get an education while serving your country.

Monthly and yearly training for National Guard members are commonly held at buildings called armories.

★ EXPLORE MORE ★

The part-time aspect of the National Guard can be a benefit. This can mean members get more time to work, go to school, or spend time with their families. However, it's important to remember National Guardsmen can be called to full-time active duty when needed.

Airmen in the air national guard follow the three core values of the U.S. Air Force. The first is "Integrity First." This means always doing what's right, even if no one is paying attention. Integrity means having the courage to make hard decisions when necessary. It also means being honest and responsible.

The second air force value is "Service Before Self." This means putting the needs of others before yours. This can mean following rules, respecting others, and having self-control.

The air force's last core value is "Excellence in All We Do." This means always doing your best and trying to get better. Airmen do this on both personal and professional levels by staying in their best shape physically, mentally, and morally. They aim for excellence in their work by keeping their skills and education strong.

EXERCISING IS ONE WAY NATIONAL GUARDSMEN WORK TO STAY IN THEIR BEST PHYSICAL SHAPE, HELPING THEM MAINTAIN THE LAST CORE VALUE OF THE AIR FORCE.

While the air force and army have different values, you can see that they are all related and come down to the same basic principles: serving others to the best of your ability, and doing so with honor, integrity, and courage. The national guard may be a part-time job, but guardsmen are expected to follow these values whether or not they're on the job.

CORE VALUES: ARMY AND AIR FORCE

ARMY
LOYALTY

DUTY

RESPECT

SELFLESS SERVICE

HONOR

INTEGRITY

PERSONAL COURAGE

AIR FORCE
INTEGRITY FIRST

SERVICE BEFORE SELF

EXCELLENCE IN ALL WE DO

THE ARMY AND AIR FORCE MAY USE DIFFERENT TERMS TO DESCRIBE THEIR VALUES, BUT MANY OF THE MEANINGS LINE UP, SUCH AS "SELFLESS SERVICE" AND "SERVICE BEFORE SELF." BOTH GROUPS STRESS THE IMPORTANCE OF INTEGRITY AND DUTY TOO.

GLOSSARY

active duty Full-time employment as a member of the military.

adversity Difficult or unfortunate conditions.

ammunition Bullets, shells, and other things fired by weapons.

artillery Large guns that shoot shells, bullets, or missiles.

aviation The act, practice, or science of flying airplanes.

bureau A specialized department or part of a department in the government.

corps A group of soldiers trained for special service.

GED Stands for general equivalency diploma, a document given to an adult who didn't finish high school but passed a test showing they have as much knowledge as a high school graduate.

hurricane A powerful storm that forms over water and causes heavy rainfall and high winds.

militia A group of citizens who organize like soldiers in order to protect themselves.

natural disaster A severe event in nature that commonly results in serious damage and deaths.

FOR MORE INFORMATION

BOOKS

Kerrigan, Michael. *Citizen Soldiers: The National Guard*. Broomall, PA: Mason Crest, 2018.

Reedy, Trent. *Divided We Fall*. New York, NY: Arthur A. Levine Books, 2014.

Shotz, Jennifer Li. *Scout: National Hero*. New York, NY: Harper, 2018.

Thompson, Jim. *My Cousin Is in the National Guard*. New York, NY: PowerKids Press, 2016.

WEBSITES

Air National Guard
www.goang.com/
Go to this site to read about the air national guard.

Army National Guard
www.nationalguard.com/
Find out about the army national guard here.

National Guard
www.nationalguard.mil/
Learn all about the U.S. National Guard on this official website of the military.

Publisher's note to educators and parents: Our editors have carefully reviewed these websites to ensure that they are suitable for students. Many websites change frequently, however, and we cannot guarantee that a site's future contents will continue to meet our high standards of quality and educational value. Be advised that students should be closely supervised whenever they access the internet.

INDEX

A

air force specialty code (AFSC), 28

Armed Services Vocational Aptitude Battery (ASVAB), 13, 14

I

Individual Ready Reserve, 12

L

Law, First Lieutenant Sylvia Marie St. Charles, 37

M

military occupational specialty (MOS), 28

motto, 23

N

National Security Act of 1947, 20

O

officer, 32, 37

P

Parsons, Captain Norma, 37

R

reserve forces, 5

S

seal, 23

song, 23

T

training, 9, 11, 28, 29, 42

V

values, 29, 36, 39, 43, 44, 45

Y

Yeager, Laura, 38